THE HUNT FOR SPRING

BY SUSAN O'HALLORAN

ILLUSTRATED BY DICK SMOLINSKI

To Krysta Kavenaugh, "adopted Sis" and editor of Marriage *magazine,*
where The Hunt for Spring *first appeared.*
Thanks, gentle Bear, for your encouragement
and ever present love and support.

Published by Riverbank Press
801 94th Avenue North, St. Petersburg, Florida 33702

Copyright © 1995 by Willowisp Press, a division of PAGES, Inc.

Printed in the United States of America

2 4 6 8 10 9 7 5 3 1

ISBN 0-87406-740-5

Once upon a time, Spring did not come. The ice and snow never melted. The flowers stayed tucked underground. The birds and the animals waited and waited, but still Spring did not come.

A young girl named Ursula and her mother lived alone in a tiny cabin. Ursula's father had died some years before. The long, long winter had made Ursula's mother very unhappy. She was so sad she hardly moved, and she rarely spoke.

One day Ursula had an idea. "Maybe," she thought, "Winter is holding Spring prisoner in the coldest part of the world. Maybe somebody will just have to go north and tell Winter to let Spring go."

At that moment, Ursula knew that she was that somebody. "Why me?" she used to say to her mother and father when they asked her to do something difficult or frightening. "Why *not* you?" they would reply. "We know you can do it." And so Ursula decided to go in search of Spring.

A neighbor promised to look after Ursula's mother. Ursula hopped on her dog sled and headed north to the land we now call the Arctic.

She drove the sled to a frozen land where there wasn't one tree. Each way Ursula turned looked the same to her. There were no villages or farms or people. The land stretched out in front of her like a frozen desert. But Ursula drove further north, determined to find Spring.

*T*hen one night a horrible storm swept across the land. Ursula tried to keep a fire going, but the snow kept falling and the wind kept howling. Ursula did not remember falling asleep. She only remembered thinking, "This is surely the end."

When Ursula woke up and opened her eyes, she saw that she was inside an igloo, a house made of ice. Next to her bed sat an old man and his young grandson. The old man looked at Ursula and smiled. "I am glad you are feeling better, my child," he said. "Tell us why you have come to this land."

"I came to find Spring," Ursula answered. "My mother and others are sick from the unending cold. Why is there no Spring?"

"Because the Lady has not ridden the Great White Bear," said the young boy. "We believe that it is a Lady who brings Spring to the land. First she tames the Great Bear. Then she rides him across the sky. Together they bring the colors of Spring to earth."

"**W**here is this Lady?" Ursula asked.

The grandfather answered, "Every hundred years a new Lady must ride the Bear. The last Lady of Spring came from our tribe. Now she must come from another."

Somehow Ursula knew that she was being chosen for this task. "How does one tame the Great Bear?" she asked.

"You must run faster than he does," the old man said. "Then the Bear will do whatever you ask."

Ursula wanted to help these good people who had saved her life. "Take me to this Bear," she said. "Let me see him. Then I will decide whether I can tame him."

They paddled for hours in the old man's boat. Then Ursula spotted the Great White Bear standing alone on a huge sheet of floating ice. This Bear was twice as big as any other bear. He bent his head near the ice and twisted his thick neck from side to side. He was listening for something. Suddenly he poked his head into a hole in the ice and pulled out a huge fish. The Great Bear ran lightly and swiftly across the ice with the big fish still in his mouth.

"No!" Ursula said. "I cannot tame such an animal. I had no idea he would be so large and powerful. I am not your Lady of Spring."

Just as she spoke those words, Ursula remembered her mother and father asking, "Why *not* you?" She thought of how badly she wanted to see her mother laugh and sing again. And that thought made her strong.

Ursula's gaze followed the Bear as it ran. "Why can the Bear run so swiftly across the ice," she asked, "when we who are so much lighter often trip and fall?"

"It is the fur between his great paws," the old man said. "The fur makes the Bear steady on the ice."

"I see," said Ursula. "Then I will do my best to tame the Bear. But we must wait until he falls asleep."

Late in the afternoon, the Great Bear settled down for a nap. Ursula moved quietly across the ice toward him. When she reached the Bear, he was sound asleep.

Ursula pulled out her hunting knife. Slowly and gently, Ursula cut the fur between the Bear's paws. Just as she finished, the Bear's eyes popped open. He let out a loud roar.

"The race is on!" Ursula shouted as she took off running across the ice. She could hear the Bear bellowing behind her and she felt his hot breath on her neck. But she kept speeding across the ice. Then she heard nothing behind her.

Ursula stopped running and turned around. The Great White Bear was slipping all over the ice. He could not run! The Bear skidded to a stop and then bent down close to the ground.

"He wants you to get on!" the grandson called to Ursula.

Ursula climbed up on the Bear's back. She held on to the fur of his neck. Then the great beast lifted her into the air. The old man and the young boy waved goodbye to Ursula. When Ursula waved her hand overhead, the colors of the rainbow sprang from her fingers.

"Strength and gentleness must always ride together," the old man said as Ursula and the Bear rode across the sky.

That day, Ursula's mother awoke to the new Spring, as did others who had waited so long for the end of Winter. And for the next one hundred years, Ursula rode the Great White Bear across the sky, bringing Spring to every land.